Once upon a time…

KISS ME!

(I'm a Prince!)

Heather McLeod
Illustrated by Brooke Kerrigan

Fitzhenry & Whiteside
www.fitzhenry.ca

ribbit.

Text copyright © 2010 Heather McLeod
Illustration copyright © 2010 Brooke Kerrigan

Published in Canada by Fitzhenry & Whiteside, 195 Allstate Parkway, Markham, Ontario L3R 4T8

Published in the United States by Fitzhenry & Whiteside, 311 Washington Street, Brighton, Massachusetts 02135

www.fitzhenry.ca   godwit@fitzhenry.ca

10 9 8 7 6 5 4 3 2

Library and Archives Canada Cataloguing in Publication
McLeod, Heather, 1971-
Kiss me! : I'm a prince / Heather McLeod ; illustrated by Brooke Kerrigan.
ISBN 978-1-55455-161-3
I. Kerrigan, Brooke II. Title.
PS8625.L4553R48 2010   jC813'.6   C2010-904388-X

U.S. Publisher Cataloging-in-Publication Data (Library of Congress Standards)
McLeod, Heather.
Kiss Me! I'm a Prince! / Heather McLeod ; illustrated by Brooke Kerrigan.
[32] p. : col. ill. ;   cm.
ISBN-13: 978-1-55455-161-3
1. Frogs – Juvenile fiction. 2. Self acceptance – Juvenile fiction.
I. Kerrigan, Brooke. II. Title.
[E] dc22   PZ7.M354Ki 2010

Fitzhenry & Whiteside acknowledges with thanks the Canada Council for the Arts, and the Ontario Arts Council for their support
of our publishing program. We acknowledge the financial support of the Government of Canada through the
Book Publishing Industry Development Program (BPIDP) for our publishing activities.

 Canada Council Conseil des Arts
for the Arts du Canada

 ONTARIO ARTS COUNCIL
CONSEIL DES ARTS DE L'ONTARIO

Cover and interior design by Kerry Designs
Cover image courtesy Brooke Kerrigan

Printed by Sheck Wah Tong in Hong Kong, China, April 2011, Job #53710

ribbit.

KISS ME!
(I'm a Prince!)

"If you kiss me, I'll turn into a prince."

But Ella didn't kiss him.

"Actually, I'm a prince already. I only look like a frog because my fairy godmother turned me into one," explained the frog. "She said it'll do me good, somehow. Anyway, go ahead. Kiss me."

And he puckered up his wide froggy lips and squeezed shut his big froggy eyes.

Ella picked him up...

...then she put him in her pocket and walked away.

Boing, boing, boing went her pocket.

"Hey, **hey, HEY!**" yelled the frog.

Ella stopped and took him out of her pocket.

"Didn't you hear what I said? If you kiss me, I'll turn into a prince!"

He puckered up his wide froggy lips and squeezed shut his big froggy eyes.

Ella put him back into her pocket and continued walking.

Boing, boing, boing went her pocket.

"Hey, **hey, HEY!**" yelled the frog.

Ella took him out of her pocket again.

"Why won't you kiss me? If you kiss me, I'll—"

"I know," interrupted Ella. "You'll turn into a prince. But then what?"

"We'll go to the palace and the king and queen—my parents—will make you a princess," promised the frog.

"And what do princes and princesses do all day?" asked Ella.

OH.

"Study mostly," said the frog. "We must learn every language in the world so when we grow up we can speak with all the other world leaders. Then there's international finance, etiquette, falconry, warfare, geography, law—"

"But when do you get to play?" asked Ella.

"Princes and princesses don't play," scoffed the frog, "unless you count studying horsemanship and fencing. I really like *those* subjects."

"What about hopscotch and Simon Says and going for a swim in the pond?" asked Ella.

"That would be unseemly," sniffed the frog. "And besides..."

"...princes wear suits and princesses wear gowns all the time. You don't get clothes like *that* dirty."

"Hmm," said Ella. "I'd rather have a talking frog."

And she put him back into her pocket and walked all the way home.

At first, the frog tried to get someone to kiss him. He'd pucker up his wide froggy lips and squeeze shut his big froggy eyes whenever anyone so much as glanced his way.

After a while, the frog gave up on getting kissed...

Does he have enough flies to eat?

...and played with Ella. They started
with hopscotch and Simon Says.

Then they went for a swim in the pond.

The frog was surprised at how much fun he was having. He even liked getting dirty.

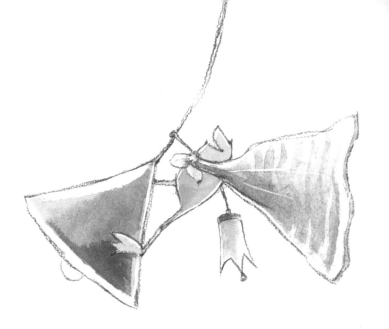

In fact, he forgot all about being *princely*—until the day a royal courtier rang the doorbell.

The courtier swept his feathered cap off his head and bowed until his nose touched the floor.

"Excuse me, miss," said the courtier. "Have you seen an, er, *unusual* frog in the neighbourhood?"

"Umm…," said Ella.

"Your majesty!" the courtier exclaimed. He swept up the frog and carried him away in a golden carriage pulled by four prancing white stallions.

Ella didn't hear from the frog for two whole weeks.

Then the royal carriage appeared in front of her house again.

"Hey," said Ella. "You're still a frog."

"Well," said the frog, "My mom and dad got everyone in the castle to kiss me. But nothing happened. My fairy godmother says only the kiss of a true friend will do—and only if I want it to. So here I am."

"Do you *want* me to kiss you?" asked Ella.

"I didn't at first," admitted the frog, "but then Mom and Dad said they'd cut back on my homework so I'll have time to play every day. I can even join your baseball team! But, frogs can't play baseball. Frogs can't do a lot of things. So yes, Ella, I want you to kiss me. *Please*?"

And Ella did.

…and they played happily ever after.